Another Little Book
of
Farmyard Tales

Heather Amery
illustrated by Stephen Cartwright

Language consultant: Betty Root
Edited by Jenny Tyler
Cover design by Hannah Ahmed

There is a little yellow duck to find in every picture.
Can you find it?

The Silly Sheepdog

This is Apple Tree Farm.

This is Mrs. Boot, the farmer. She has two children, called Poppy and Sam, and a dog called Rusty.

Ted works on Apple Tree Farm.

He has just bought a sheepdog to help him with the sheep. The sheepdog is called Patch.

3

Poppy, Sam and Rusty say hello to Patch.

"Come on, Patch," says Sam. "We'll show you all the animals on our farm."

First they look at the hens.

Patch jumps into the hen run and chases the hens.
They are frightened and fly up onto their house.

"Now we'll go and see the cows."

Patch runs into the field and barks at the cows.
But they just stand and stare at him.

6

Then they look at the pigs.

Patch jumps into the pig pen and chases all the pigs
into their little house.

Sam shouts at Patch.

"Come here, you silly thing. You're meant to be
a sheepdog. Ted will have to send you back."

8

They go to the sheep field.

"Look," says Sam. "One sheep is missing." "Yes, it's that naughty Woolly again," says Ted.

"Where's Patch going?" says Sam.

Patch runs away across the field. Ted, Sam, Poppy and Rusty run after him.

Patch dives through the hedge.

Patch barks and barks. "What has he found?"
says Sam. They all go to look.

Patch has found a boy.

The boy pats Patch. "Hello," he says. "I wondered who bought you when my dad sold his farm."

The boy has found a sheep.

"There's Woolly," says Sam. "I found her on the
road," says the boy. "I was bringing her back."

The boy whistles to Patch.

Patch chases Woolly back through the gate.
She runs into the field with the other sheep.

14

Ted stares in surprise.

"Patch doesn't do anything I tell him," says Ted.
"You don't know how to whistle," says the boy.

Patch runs back to them.

"You must teach me how to whistle to Patch,"
says Ted. "He's not a silly dog after all," says Sam.

16

Kitten's Day Out

This is Apple Tree Farm.

This is Mrs. Boot, the farmer. She has two children, called Poppy and Sam, and a dog called Rusty.

Ted works on the farm.

He is helping Mr. Bran, the truck driver. Mr. Bran
has brought some sacks of food for the cows.

They say goodbye to Mr. Bran.

Mr. Bran waves as he drives his truck out
of the farmyard. Ted and Poppy wave back.

20

"Where's my kitten?"

"Where's Fluff?" says Sam. They all look
everywhere for Fluff. But they can't find her.

21

"Perhaps she jumped on the truck."

"Take my car and go after the truck, Ted," says
Mrs. Boot. They jump in the car and drive off.

Ted stops the car at the crossroads.

"Which way did Mr. Bran go?" says Ted. "There's a truck," says Sam. "It's just going around the bend."

23

Ted drives down a steep hill.

"Look out Ted," says Poppy. There's a stream at the bottom. The car splashes into the water.

The car stops in the stream.

"Water in the engine," says Ted. "I'll have to push."
"We'll never find the truck now," says Sam.

Ted looks inside the car.

He mops up all the water. Soon he gets the car
to start again. They drive on to look for the truck.

There are lots of sheep on the road.

"The sheep came out of the field. Someone left the gate open," says Ted. "We must get them back."

Ted, Poppy and Sam round up the sheep.

They drive them back into the field. Ted shuts the gate. "Come on, we must hurry," says Sam.

28

"Stop, Ted, there's a truck."

"I'm sure that's Mr. Bran's truck in that farmyard," says Sam. Ted drives in to see.

"It's the wrong truck."

"Oh dear," says Poppy. "It's not Mr. Bran, and that's not Mr. Bran's truck."

Ted drives them home.

"We'll never find my kitten now," says Sam.
"I'm sure she'll turn up," says Poppy.

There's a surprise at Apple Tree Farm.

"Here's your kitten," says Mr. Bran. "She's been in my truck all day and now I've brought her home."

The New Pony

This is Apple Tree Farm.

This is Mrs. Boot, the farmer. She has two children, called Poppy and Sam, and a dog called Rusty.

Mr. Boot, Poppy and Sam go for a walk.

They see a new pony. "She belongs to Mr. Stone, who's just bought Old Gate Farm," says Mr. Boot.

The pony looks sad.

Her coat is rough and dirty. She looks hungry.
It looks as though no one takes care of her.

Poppy tries to stroke the pony.

"She's not very friendly," says Sam. "Mr. Stone says she's bad tempered," says Mr. Boot.

Poppy feeds the pony.

Every day, Poppy takes her apples and carrots.
But she always stays on the other side of the gate.

One day, Poppy takes Sam with her.

They cannot see the pony anywhere. The field looks empty. "Where is she?" says Sam.

Poppy and Sam open the gate.

Rusty runs into the field. Poppy and Sam are a
bit scared. "We must find the pony," says Poppy.

"There she is," says Sam.

The pony has caught her head collar in the fence.
She has been eating the grass on the other side.

Poppy and Sam run home to Mr. Boot.

"Please come and help us, Dad," says Poppy. "The pony is caught in the fence. She will hurt herself."

Mr. Boot walks up to the pony.

He unhooks the pony's head collar from the fence.
"She's not hurt," says Mr. Boot.

"The pony's chasing us."

"Quick, run," says Sam. "It's all right," says Poppy, patting the pony. "She just wants to be friends."

They see an angry man. It is Mr. Stone.

"Leave my pony alone," says Mr. Stone. "And get out of my field." He waves his stick at Poppy.

The pony is afraid of Mr. Stone.

Mr. Stone tries to hit the pony with his stick. "I'm going to get rid of that nasty animal," he says.

Poppy grabs his arm.

"You mustn't hit the pony," she cries. "Come on Poppy," says Mr. Boot. "Let's go home."

Next day, there's a surprise for Poppy.

The pony is at Apple Tree Farm. "We've bought her
for you," says Mrs. Boot. "Thank you," says Poppy.

The Grumpy Goat

This is Apple Tree Farm.

This is Mrs. Boot, the farmer. She has two children, called Poppy and Sam, and a dog called Rusty.

Ted works on the farm.

He tells Poppy and Sam to clean the goat's shed.
"Will she let us?" asks Sam. "She's so grumpy now."

51

Gertie the goat chases Sam.

She butts him with her head. He nearly falls over.
Sam, Poppy and Rusty run out through the gate.

Poppy shuts the gate.

They must get Gertie out of her pen so they can get to her shed. "I have an idea," says Sam.

Sam gets a bag of bread.

"Come on, Gertie," says Sam. "Nice bread."
Gertie eats it and the bag, but stays in her pen.

"Let's try some fresh grass," says Poppy.

Poppy pulls up some grass and drops it by the gate. Gertie eats it but trots back into her pen.

"I have another idea," says Sam.

"Gertie doesn't butt Ted. She wouldn't butt me if I looked like Ted," says Sam. He runs off again.

Sam comes back wearing Ted's clothes.

He has found Ted's old coat and hat. Sam goes into the pen but Gertie still butts him.

"I'll get a rope," says Poppy.

They go into the pen. Poppy tries to throw the
rope over Gertie's head. She misses.

Gertie chases them all.

Rusty runs out of the pen and Gertie follows him.
"She's out!" shouts Sam. "Quick, shut the gate."

Sam and Poppy clean out Gertie's shed.

They sweep up the old straw and put it in the
wheelbarrow. They spread out fresh straw.

Poppy opens the gate.

"Come on, Gertie. You can go back now," says Sam.
Gertie trots back into her pen.

"You are a grumpy old goat," says Poppy.

"We've cleaned out your shed and you're still grumpy," says Sam. "Grumpy Gertie."

Next morning, they meet Ted.

"Come and look at Gertie now," says Ted. They all
go to the goat pen.

Gertie has a little kid.

"Oh, isn't it sweet," says Poppy. "Gertie doesn't look grumpy now," says Sam.

The
Snow Storm

This is Apple Tree Farm.

This is Mrs. Boot, the farmer. She has two children, called Poppy and Sam, and a dog called Rusty.

In the night there was a big snow storm.

In the morning, it is still snowing. "You must wrap up warm," says Mrs. Boot to Poppy and Sam.

Ted works on the farm.

He helps Mrs. Boot look after the animals.
He gives them food and water every day.

"Come and help me," calls Ted.

"Where are you going?" says Poppy. "I'm taking this hay to the sheep," says Ted.

Poppy and Sam pull the hay.

They go out of the farmyard with Ted. They walk
to the gate of the sheep field.

"Where are the sheep?" says Sam.

"They are all covered with snow," says Ted.
"We'll have to find them," says Poppy.

They brush the snow off the sheep.

Ted, Poppy and Sam give each sheep lots of hay.
"They've got nice warm coats," says Sam.

Poppy counts the sheep.

"There are only six sheep. One is missing," says
Poppy. "It's that naughty Woolly," says Ted.

They look for Woolly.

They walk around the snowy field. "Rusty, good dog, find Woolly," calls Sam.

Rusty runs across the field.

Ted, Poppy and Sam run after him. Rusty barks
at the thick hedge.

Ted looks under the hedge.

"Can you see anything?" says Sam. "Yes, Woolly is hiding in there. Clever Rusty," says Ted.

"Come on, Woolly."

"Let me help you out, old girl," says Ted.
Carefully he pulls Woolly out of the hedge.

"There's something else!"

"Look, I can see something moving," says Sam.
"What is it, Ted?" says Poppy.

Ted lifts out a tiny lamb.

"Woolly has had a lamb," he says. "We'll take it and Woolly to the barn. They'll be warm there."

Poppy rides home.

She holds the lamb. "What a surprise!" she says.
"Good old Woolly."

Surprise Visitors

This is Apple Tree Farm.

This is Mrs. Boot, the farmer. She has two children, called Poppy and Sam, and a dog called Rusty.

Today is Saturday.

Mrs. Boot, Poppy and Sam are having breakfast.
"Why are the cows so noisy?" asks Sam.

They all run out to the field.

The cows are running around the field. They are
scared. A big balloon is floating over the trees.

"It's a hot air balloon."

"It's coming down," says Mrs. Boot. "It's going to land in our field." The balloon hits the ground.

85

There are two people in it.

"Where are we?" asks the man. "This is Apple Tree
Farm. You frightened our cows," says Mrs. Boot.

The man climbs out.

"I'm Alice and this is Tim," says the woman.
"We ran out of gas. Sorry about your cows."

"A truck is following us."

"There it is now," says Alice. "Our friend is bringing more cylinders of gas for the balloon."

Alice helps to unload the truck.

Tim unloads the empty cylinders. Then he puts the new ones into the balloon's basket.

They blow up the balloon.

Poppy and Sam help Tim hold open the balloon.
A fan blows hot air into it. It gets bigger and bigger.

"Would you like a ride?"

"Oh, yes please," says Poppy. "Just a little one," says Tim. "The truck will bring you back."

91

Mrs. Boot, Poppy and Sam climb in.

Tim lights the gas burner. The big flames make
a loud noise. "Hold on tight," says Alice.

The balloon goes up.

Slowly it leaves the ground. Tim turns off the
burner. "The wind is blowing us along," he says.

The balloon floats along.

"I can see our farm down there," says Poppy.
"Look, there's Alice in the truck," says Sam.

"We're going down now," says Tim.

The balloon floats down and the basket lands in a field. Mrs. Boot helps Poppy and Sam out.

"Thank you very much."

They wave as the balloon takes off again.
"We were flying," says Sam.

Market Day

This is Apple Tree Farm.

This is Mrs. Boot, the farmer. She has two children, called Poppy and Sam, and a dog called Rusty.

Today is market day.

Mrs. Boot puts the trailer on the car. Poppy and
Sam put a wire crate in the trailer.

They drive to the market.

Mrs. Boot, Poppy and Sam walk past cows, sheep and
pigs. They go to the shed which has cages of birds.

100

There are different kinds of geese.

"Let's look in all the cages," says Mrs. Boot.
"I want four nice young geese."

"There are four nice white ones."

"They look nice and friendly," says Poppy.
"Yes, they are just what I want," says Mrs. Boot.

A woman is selling the geese.

"How much are the four white ones?" asks Mrs. Boot. "I'll buy them, please." She pays for them.

"We'll come back later."

"Let's look at the other birds," says Sam. There are cages with hens, chicks, ducks and pigeons.

"Look at the poor little duck."

"It's lonely," says Poppy. "Please may I buy it?
I can pay for it with my own money."

"Yes, you can buy it."

"We'll get it when we come back for the geese,"
says Mrs. Boot. Poppy pays the man for the duck.

Mrs. Boot brings the crate.

Poppy opens the lid. The woman passes the geese to Mrs. Boot. She puts them in the crate.

One of the geese runs away.

A goose jumps out of the crate just before Sam
shuts the door. It runs very fast out of the shed.

"Catch that goose."

Mrs. Boot, Poppy and Sam run after the goose.
The goose jumps through an open car door.

"Now we've got it," says Sam.

But a woman opens a door on the other side.
The goose jumps out of the car and runs away.

"Run after it," says Mrs. Boot.

The goose runs into the plant tent.
"There it is," says Sam, and picks it up.

"Let's go home," says Mrs. Boot.

"I've got my geese now." "And I've got my duck,"
says Poppy. "Markets are fun," says Sam.

Camping Out

This is Apple Tree Farm.

This is Mrs. Boot, the farmer. She has two children, called Poppy and Sam, and a dog called Rusty.

114

A car stops at the gate.

A man, a woman and a boy get out.
"Hello," says the man. "May we camp on your farm?"

"Yes, you can camp over there."

"We'll show you the way," says Mr. Boot.
The campers follow in the car.

The campers put up their tent.

Poppy and Sam help them. They take chairs,
a table, a cooking stove and food out of the car.

Then they all go to the farmhouse.

Mrs. Boot gives the campers a bucket of water
and some milk. Poppy and Sam bring some eggs.

"Can we go camping?"

"Please Dad, can we put up our tent too?"
says Poppy. "Oh yes, please Dad," says Sam.

Mr. Boot gets out the tent.

Poppy and Sam try to put up the little blue tent
but it keeps falling down. At last it is ready.

"Come and have supper."

"Then you can go to the tent," says Mrs. Boot.
"But you must wash and brush your teeth first."

Poppy and Sam go to the tent.

"It's not dark yet," says Sam. "Come on, Rusty.
You can come camping with us," says Poppy.

Poppy and Sam go to bed.

They crawl into the tent and tie up the door.
Then they wriggle into their sleeping bags.

123

"What's that noise?"

Sam sits up. "There's something walking around outside the tent," says Sam. "What is it?"

124

Poppy looks out of the tent.

"It's only Daisy, the cow," she says. "She must have strayed into this field. She's so nosy."

Daisy looks into the tent.

Rusty barks at her. Daisy is scared. She tries to
back away but the tent catches on her head.

Daisy pulls at the tent.

She pulls it down and runs off with it. Rusty chases her. Poppy and Sam run back to the house.

127

Mr. Boot opens the door.